for Sylvia

Barefoot Beginners
an imprint of
Barefoot Books, Inc.
41 Schermerhorn Street, Suite 145
Brooklyn, New York
11201-4845

This book is printed on 100% acid-free paper

Cover design by Jennie Hoare
Printed and bound in Singapore by Tien Wah Press Pte Ltd

ISBN 1 902283 45 7
1 3 5 7 9 8 6 4 2

PETER'S PATCHWORK DREAM

WILLEMIEN MIN

BAREFOOT BOOKS

Peter was not feeling well. His head ached and his eyes were sore.
"You need lots to drink and plenty of sleep!" said his mom. "Then you'll feel better in the morning."

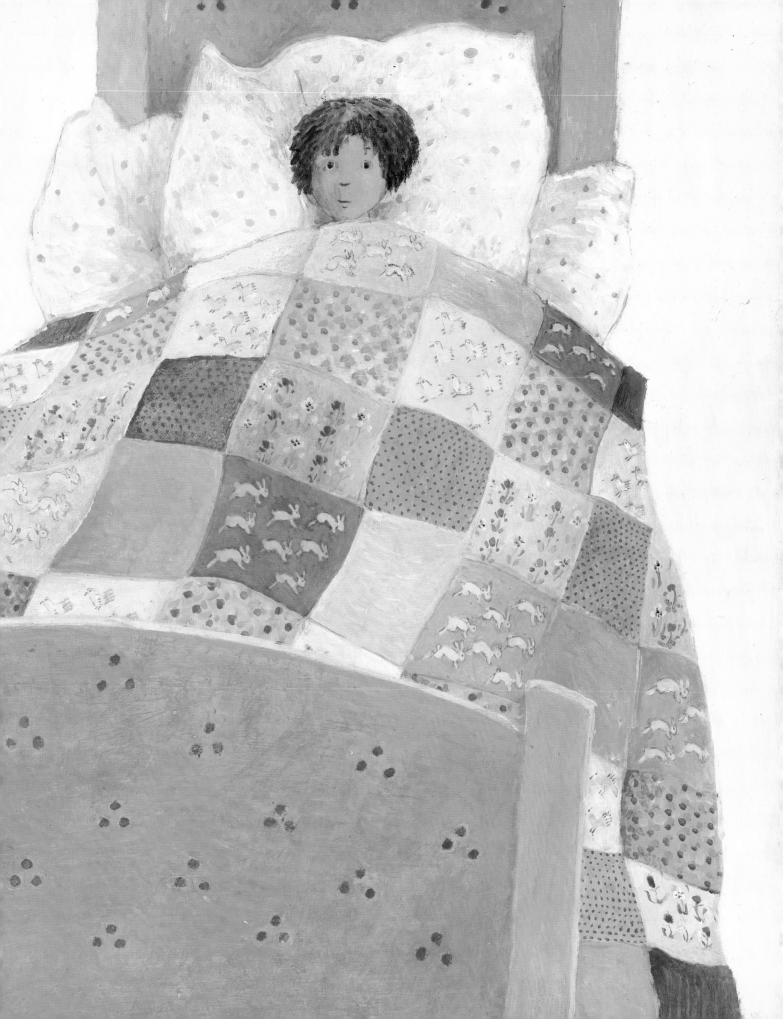

How boring, thought Peter. His mom was busy and no one came to visit him. Then his eyes started to wander over his quilt, with its bright patchwork fields.

"I think I'll go for a walk,"
Peter said to himself. So off
he went, past apple trees and
wild flowers and bushes that
were bright with berries.
He was in a great big garden.

Peter started to pick the berries.
"Mmmm!" he said, "These are so
sweet and juicy! One for me, one for
Mom, one for me, one for Dad…"
Soon his basket was full to the brim.

But Peter was not the only one who liked the berries! The birds thought they were delicious, too. "Hey!" cried Peter. "That's my basket! Look out! Oh no…all right, you can eat the berries. I'll find something else. Let me see…"

"Apples! I'll take home some of these fat apples. One, two, three…now my basket is full again — but it's very heavy! Aha! Who's waiting for me over there?"

"Hello, bunnies! Would you like some apples? Here's one for you, and here's one for me. You're very tame, aren't you? Would you like to come on an adventure with me?"

"All aboard! We're sailing over the sea. Careful — don't rock the boat! Hold on tight…whoops! Too late. Never mind; we'll soon be dry again."

"These flowers look thirsty. Here!
Now you're wet, too. What beautiful
flowers you are! I wish I could take
you home with me."

"What a wonderful day I've had!
Take care, bunnies, take care, birds.
I'm going home now, before it gets
dark. Listen! My mom is calling me."

"Peter!" called his mom, "Look who's here!"
Peter sat up in bed and listened. He could
hear her talking to someone at the front door:
"Oh! How kind of you all to come round!
Peter has been on his own all day. He has
been so bored! Poor, sick Peter!"

But poor, sick Peter was not so sick anymore! He was hopping and skipping all over his patchwork quilt. Poor, sick Peter was better again!

BAREFOOT BOOKS publishes high-quality picture books for
children of all ages and specializes in the work of artists and writers from
many cultures. If you have enjoyed this book and would like to receive a copy
of our current catalog, please write to our New York office: Barefoot Books,
41 Schermerhorn Street, Suite 145, Brooklyn, New York, NY 11201-4845
email: ussales@barefoot-books.com   website: www.barefoot-books.com